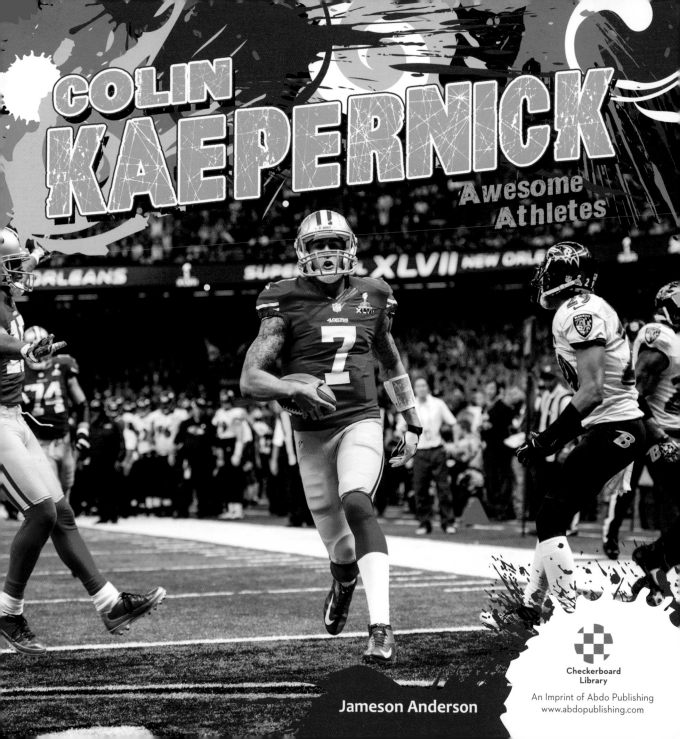

COLIN KAEPERNICK

Awesome Athletes

Jameson Anderson

Checkerboard
Library

An Imprint of Abdo Publishing
www.abdopublishing.com

www.abdopublishing.com

Published by Abdo Publishing, a division of ABDO, PO Box 398166, Minneapolis, Minnesota 55439.
Copyright © 2015 by Abdo Consulting Group, Inc. International copyrights reserved in all countries.
No part of this book may be reproduced in any form without written permission from the publisher.
Checkerboard Library™ is a trademark and logo of Abdo Publishing.

Printed in the United States of America, North Mankato, Minnesota.
052014
092014

THIS BOOK CONTAINS
RECYCLED MATERIALS

Cover Photo: AP Images
Interior Photos: Alamy pp. 9, 11, 13, 20, 27, 29; AP Images pp. 15, 17, 19, 25;
     Getty Images pp. 1, 5, 7, 23

Series Coordinator: Tamara L. Britton
Editor: Rochelle Baltzer
Art Direction: Neil Klinepier

Library of Congress Cataloging-in-Publication Data

Anderson, Jameson.
  Colin Kaepernick / Jameson Anderson.
     pages cm. -- (Awesome athletes)
  Includes index.
  ISBN 978-1-62403-331-5
1. Kaepernick, Colin, 1987---Juvenile literature. 2. Football players--United States--Biography
--Juvenile literature. I. Title.
  GV939.K25A53 2015
  796.332092--dc23
  [B]
                         2014000110

TABLE OF CONTENTS

SURPRISE SUPERSTAR

Colin Kaepernick had gone almost a year and a half without playing much football. Sure, he was a quarterback in the **National Football League (NFL)**. But, he was just a backup for the San Francisco 49ers. He didn't play often. It was hard for a man who had been a star player since he was a boy.

But that would change halfway through the 2012 season. During a game against the St. Louis Rams, the starting quarterback was injured. It was Kaepernick's time to shine. He led the 49ers to a tie. Kaepernick impressed coach Jim Harbaugh enough that he became the starting quarterback.

Kaepernick led his team to a 12–4 regular season. In the **playoffs**, the 49ers defeated the Green Bay Packers and the Atlanta Falcons. They would meet the Baltimore

Kaepernick took over on the 49ers' second drive in the second quarter against the Rams. He went 11 for 17 for 117 yards (107 m) and rushed eight times for 66 yards (60 m). He never lost the starting position.

Ravens in the **Super Bowl**. Kaepernick had shown that his coach's confidence was not misplaced. But could he deliver a Super Bowl win?

HIGHLIGHT REEL

Colin Rand Kaepernick was born in Milwaukee, Wisconsin.

1987

The San Francisco 49ers selected Kaepernick with the 36th pick in the second round of the NFL Draft.

2011

Kaepernick led the 49ers past the Atlanta Hawks and won the NFC Championship.

2012

2010

Kaepernick graduated from the University of Nevada–Reno.

2012

Kaepernick took over when Alex Smith was injured. He never lost the starting position.

2013

In Kaepernick's tenth NFL start, the 49ers met the Baltimore Ravens in Super Bowl XLVII but lost 34–31.

COLIN KAEPERNICK

DOB: November 3, 1987
Ht: 6'4"
Wt: 230
Position: QB
Number: 7

CAREER STATISTICS:

Passing Yards:	5,046
Passing Touchdowns:	31
Rushing Yards:	937
Rushing Touchdowns:	9
Quarterback Rating:	93.8

AWARDS:
NFC Championship: 2012

YOUNG COLIN

Colin Rand Kaepernick was born in Milwaukee, Wisconsin, on November 3, 1987. Rick and Teresa Kaepernick lived in Fond du Lac, Wisconsin. Rick worked at a cheese factory. Teresa was a nurse.

The Kaepernicks had two children, a son Kyle and a daughter Devon. The couple had two other sons. But, they had heart problems. Both boys died when they were babies.

The Kaepernicks decided not to have more children. But they still wanted another child. So, they decided to adopt. The Kaepernicks did not care what race their adopted child was. They were not concerned about the baby's health. They just wanted another child. The Kaepernicks adopted Colin when he was five weeks old.

Colin's mom and dad, Rick and Teresa Kaepernick

A TALENTED ATHLETE

When Colin was four years old, the Kaepernicks moved to Turlock, California. There, Colin joined his first youth sports leagues. He played football and baseball.

On his football team, Colin played kicker and on the defensive line. When he was nine years old, he started as quarterback. On his baseball team, Colin was the pitcher.

Colin was so good at both sports that his parents and friends called him "Bo." Bo Jackson was a professional athlete who played football and baseball. Colin's parents still sometimes call him "Bo" even though he is grown up!

For a fourth-grade assignment, Colin had to write a letter to his future self. Colin wrote that he wanted to

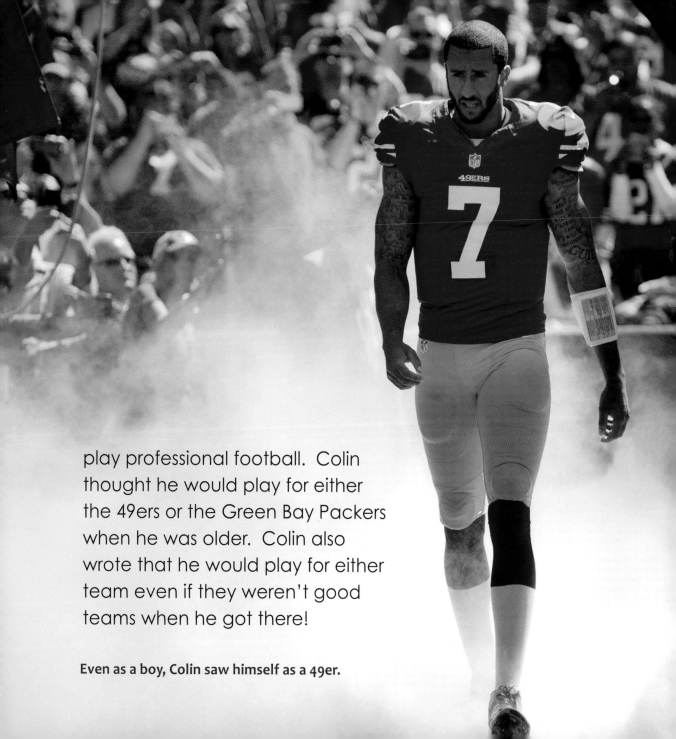

play professional football. Colin thought he would play for either the 49ers or the Green Bay Packers when he was older. Colin also wrote that he would play for either team even if they weren't good teams when he got there!

Even as a boy, Colin saw himself as a 49er.

FOCUSED ON FOOTBALL

Colin attended John H. Pitman High School in Turlock. There, Colin excelled in more than just football. As a pitcher on the Pride's baseball team, he could pitch fastballs at more than 90 miles per hour (145 km/h). He also earned good grades.

With the speed of his fastball, many thought Colin could have a career in **Major League Baseball (MLB)**. But Colin focused on football. He led the Pride to the school's first state **playoff** victory.

As Colin's high school career came to an end, his father and brother made a video showing Colin's best plays. They sent it to 100 college football coaches. But none offered Colin a football **scholarship**. Colin was 6 feet 6 inches (2 m 15 cm) tall, yet weighed just 170

pounds (77 kg). Many coaches believed that he was too thin to play college football. They believed Colin would be easily injured.

Meanwhile, Colin received baseball **scholarship** offers from the University of Tennessee, Arizona State University, and Notre Dame. Colin declined these offers. He remained focused on football.

MLB scouts believed Colin had a future in professional baseball. In the 2009 MLB draft, the Chicago Cubs selected him with the 1,310th pick in the forty-third round.

LEADER OF THE PACK

In 2006, Colin's patience and commitment to his dream paid off. He received a **scholarship** from the University of Nevada–Reno. Colin **redshirted** his first year with the Wolf Pack. The coaches wanted him to start at safety and work into the quarterback position.

In 2007, Wolf Pack quarterback Nick Graziano was injured in a game against Fresno State. Colin got a chance to play, and he made it count. He threw for 384 yards (351 m) and four touchdowns. He was named the starting quarterback for the rest of the year.

In 2008, Colin became the fifth player in college football history to pass for 2,000 yards (1,829 m) and rush for 1,000 yards (914 m) in the same season. He was named Most Valuable Player his sophomore and junior years. As a junior, Colin became the first player in college football history to reach 2,000 yards passing and 1,000 yards rushing two years in a row.

But Colin wasn't done. He put up the same numbers his senior year. Colin remains the only player to hold this record three years in a row.

As a senior, Colin threw for 192 yards (176 m) and a touchdown as he led the Wolf Pack to a 20–13 victory over the Eagles of Boston College in the 2011 Kraft Fight Hunger Bowl.

THE NFL

Kaepernick graduated from Nevada–Reno in December 2010. The 2011 **NFL Draft** began on April 28 the following year. Professional football experts expected that Kaepernick would be drafted late in the first round or early in the second round.

There were twelve quarterbacks in that year's draft. Kaepernick wasn't the highest rated in the group. Five quarterbacks were drafted before him.

But Kaepernick's **perseverance** was rewarded. The San Francisco 49ers traded three picks in the draft to move up and draft him. Kaepernick was the thirty-sixth pick in the second round of the draft. He signed a four-year, $5.124 million contract his **rookie** year.

FUN FACT

OF THE FIVE QUARTERBACKS THAT WENT BEFORE KAEPERNICK IN THE 2011 DRAFT—CAM NEWTON, JAKE LOCKER, BLAINE GABBERT, CHRISTIAN PONDER, AND ANDY DALTON—NONE HAS LED HIS TEAM TO A SUPER BOWL. IN FACT, IN MARCH 2014, GABBERT WAS TRADED TO THE 49ERS. HE BECAME KAEPERNICK'S BACKUP!

At the 2011 NFL Scouting Combine, Kaepernick set a combine record when he threw a 59-mile-an-hour (95-km/h) pass.

SURPRISE STARTER

Kaepernick spent the 2011 season as backup quarterback. He played in three games. He completed three of five passes for 35 yards (32 m). The 49ers made it to the NFC Championship game, but were defeated by the New York Giants.

The 2012 season began with Kaepernick still in the backup role. But that changed on November 11 during a game against the St. Louis Rams. Starting quarterback Alex Smith scrambled from the **pocket** and was hit by Rams **linebacker** Jo-Lonn Dunbar. Smith sustained a **concussion**, and Kaepernick took over at quarterback. The game ended in a 24–24 tie.

Some fans thought Smith should be the starting quarterback when he recovered. But 49ers head coach Jim Harbaugh did not agree. He wanted to keep

Kaepernick runs for seven yards (6 m) and a touchdown against the Rams. He had eight carries for 66 yards (60 m) in the game.

Kaepernicking after a touchdown against the Packers. It was Kaepernick's first playoff game.

Kaepernick on the field as much as possible. Both the coach and Kaepernick knew that hard work would lead to success for both the player and the team.

Kaepernick put in extra hours to remain the starting quarterback. He came to practice early and stayed late. He finished the season 136-for-218 for 1,814 yards (1,659 m) with 10 touchdowns and only three **interceptions**. The 49ers finished with an 11–4–1 record.

That year, Kaepernick led the 49ers to the **playoffs**. The 49ers defeated the Green Bay Packers 45–31. Kaepernick rushed for a record-breaking 181 yards (165 m). He had 444 total yards (406 m) of offense and four touchdowns.

The 49ers advanced to the NFC Championship game. There, the team defeated the Atlanta Falcons 28–24, with Kaepernick going 16 of 21 for 233 yards (213 m) and one touchdown. With this victory, the 49ers were headed to the **Super Bowl**.

KAEPERNICKING

KAEPERNICK'S TATTOOS INCLUDE THE WORD *FAITH* ON HIS THROWING ARM'S BICEPS. AFTER THROWING A TOUCHDOWN, HE CELEBRATES BY KISSING THIS BICEPS. FANS CALL THIS KAEPERNICKING.

THE SUPER BOWL

On Sunday, February 3, 2013, the 49ers faced the Baltimore Ravens in **Super Bowl** XLVII. The game was held at the Mercedes-Benz Superdome in New Orleans, Louisiana. The 49ers were down 21–6 at halftime. It looked as if Baltimore would take home the Vince Lombardi Trophy.

Things looked worse for the 49ers when Ravens wide receiver Jacoby Jones returned the second half kickoff 108 yards (99 m) for a touchdown. It was the longest kickoff return in **NFL** history and increased the Ravens' advantage to 28–6.

On the next drive, the 49ers began their comeback. Then, the Superdome's electricity went out. The arena was almost dark for 34 minutes. During the break, the 49ers discussed their game plan.

FUN FACT THE BALTIMORE RAVENS' HEAD COACH WAS JOHN HARBAUGH, 49ERS COACH JIM HARBAUGH'S BROTHER. IT WAS THE FIRST TIME IN SUPER BOWL HISTORY THAT TWO BROTHERS COACHED THE GAME. FANS CALLED THE GAME "THE HARBOWL."

Super Bowl XLVII was Kaepernick's tenth NFL start.

When the lights came back on, the 49ers came roaring back. A quick touchdown from Kaepernick to receiver Michael Crabtree closed the gap to 28–13. Running back Frank Gore scored from six yards (5 m) out to make it 28–20. Then, kicker David Akers kicked a field goal. The 49ers scored two touchdowns and a field goal in just over four minutes!

The Ravens scored first in the fourth quarter, kicking a field goal to widen the gap to 31–23. Kaepernick ran for a 15-yard (14-m) touchdown. But a **two-point conversion** failed, and the score was 31–29. The 49ers scored two more points on a **safety**, but were not able to score on the last play of the game.

Kaepernick's play inspired his team. Both the offense and the defense played better in the game's second half. Though Kaepernick was 16 of 28 for 302 yards (276 m), the 49ers lost the game 34–31.

Kaepernick was upset after the loss. He had led his team to the **Super Bowl** and had come up short. Kaepernick gave himself one week of rest. Then, he went back to work.

Wide receiver Michael Crabtree celebrates
Kaepernick's fourth-quarter touchdown.

A NEAR MISS

Heading into the 2013 season, the 49ers traded Alex Smith to the Kansas City Chiefs. Kaepernick was then the undisputed leader of the team.

The 49ers started 2013 off strong. At the **bye**, they had lost only two games. The team finished the season with six wins in a row to finish 12–4 and once again reached the **playoffs**. Kaepernick finished the season an impressive 243 of 416 for 3,197 yards (2,923 m).

The 49ers defeated the Green Bay Packers and the Carolina Panthers in the playoffs. Once again the team reached the NFC Championship game. There, the 49ers faced the Seattle Seahawks. The Seahawks had defeated the 49ers in Week 2. This time, the 49ers needed a win to reach the **Super Bowl**.

The 49ers jumped to a 10–0 lead in the game. But Kaepernick threw two **interceptions** and lost two **fumbles**. And, the 49ers defense had a hard time stopping

Seahawks quarterback Russell Wilson. Wilson went 16 of 25 for 215 yards (197 m) and a touchdown. The Seahawks scored 10 unanswered points in the fourth quarter and won the game 17–23.

Seahawk Michael Bennett ran this Kaepernick fumble back 17 yards (16 m).

INTO THE FUTURE

Kaepernick took the blame for the loss against the Seahawks. But Coach Harbaugh did not agree. He believed Kaepernick had played a good game.

Kaepernick did not waste time in the off-season. He traveled to Florida and began training and conditioning for the next season's schedule. On June 4, 2014, the 49ers made Kaepernick their quarterback of the future. He signed a new six-year, $126 million contract.

In just one and a half seasons, Kaepernick led his team to two conference championship games and a **Super Bowl**. As he gains experience, his achievements are sure to be even greater. Colin Kaepernick is moving ahead into a bright future.

GIVING BACK

TO HONOR HIS TWO BROTHERS WHO DIED FROM HEART DEFECTS, KAEPERNICK SUPPORTS CAMP TAYLOR. CAMP TAYLOR OFFERS SUMMER CAMPS FOR KIDS WHO HAVE HEART DISEASE.

Kaepernick hanging out with kids from Camp Taylor.

GLOSSARY

bye - a week during which a team does not play a game.

concussion - a brain injury caused by a blow to the head.

draft - an event during which sports teams choose new players. Choosing new players is known as drafting them.

fumble - to lose hold of a football while handling or running with it.

interception - a pass thrown by a quarterback that is caught by a player on the opposing team.

linebacker - a defensive player who can defend both running and passing plays.

Major League Baseball - the highest level of professional baseball. It is made up of the American League (AL) and the National League (NL).

National Football League - the highest level of professional football. It is made up of the American Football Conference (AFC) and the National Football Conference (NFC).

perseverance - the quality that allows a person to keep trying to do something even though it is difficult.

playoffs - a series of games that determine which team will win a championship.

pocket - an area in which the quarterback stands while the offense protects the player from the defense.

redshirt - to limit a college athlete's participation in a sport for one school year.

rookie - a first-year player in a professional sport.

safety - a scoring play that results in two points.

scholarship - money or aid given to help a student continue his or her studies.

Super Bowl - the annual National Football League (NFL) championship game. It is played by the winners of the American and National Conferences.

two-point conversion - a two-point score in football. It is made by getting the ball in the opponent's end zone after a touchdown has been made.

WEBSITES

To learn more about Awesome Athletes, visit **booklinks.abdopublishing.com**. These links are routinely monitored and updated to provide the most current information available.

INDEX